Running Girl

The Diary of **Ebonee Rose**

Sharon Bell Mathis

Browndeer Press
Harcourt Brace & Company
San Diego   New York   London

Quote on page iii from *Bronzeville Boys and Girls*
by Gwendolyn Brooks, copyright 1956 by Gwendolyn Brooks
Blakely. Used by kind permission of the author.

Photo Credits

page iv: Allsport (Hulton Deutsch); page 10: UPI/Corbis-
Bettmann; pages 15, 29, 33, 41, and 49: Allsport (Tony Duffy);
pages 17 and 27: Allsport (Mike Powell); pages 18 and 52:
AP/Wide World Photos; page 24: Allsport (Bob Martin);
page 45: Allsport (USOC).

Browndeer Press is a registered trademark of
Harcourt Brace & Company.

Library of Congress Cataloging-in-Publication Data
Mathis, Sharon Bell.
Running girl: the diary of Ebonee Rose/Sharon Bell Mathis.
p. cm.
"Browndeer Press."
Summary: In her diary Ebonee Rose records her passion
for running, her desire to be like the great African American
women athletes who have come before her, and her
preparations for the All-City Meet.
ISBN 0-15-200674-5
[1. Running—Fiction. 2. Track and field—Fiction.
3. Afro-Americans—Fiction. 4. Diaries—Fiction.] I. Title.
PZ7.M4284Ru 1997
[Fic]—dc20 96-29066

The display type was set in Limehouse Script.
The text type was set in Minion.
Color separations by United Graphic
Printed and bound by Tien Wah Press, Singapore
This book was printed on totally chlorine-free
Nymolla Matte Art paper.
Production supervision by Stanley Redfern
Designed by Lydia D'moch

First edition
A C E F D B

Printed in Singapore

For my granddaughter,
Stacia Bishayé Mathis

my sister,
Marcia Cynthia Bell,
sprinter (the Police Athletic League, New York):
100 meters, 400-meter relay

my grandnieces,
Nöel Loren Rutledge
and Jerron Alexandria Rutledge

my nephew,
Terrance Heyward

a young athlete,
Tola Christopher Kasali

and for all children—everywhere—who love to run

What good is sun If I can't run?

GWENDOLYN BROOKS,
"PAULETTE"

"I love[d] the feeling of freedom in running, . . . that the only person I'm really competing against is me."

WILMA RUDOLPH

Wilma Rudolph

Sunday, June 1

Dear Diary,

You are new and beautiful in your kente cloth cover. Cool, cool! But I never thought about you until this morning.

I'm dressed up and on my way to church, but there are things I have to say (I mean <u>write</u>).

Daddy is a real writer, not me. He's a journalist. Last year he bought you for my birthday present. He wanted me to keep my notes and poems about running together in a book. Usually I wrote my track stuff on scraps of paper, which I either lost or stuffed in my sock drawer. I stuck you in my sock drawer, too. I didn't need you then.

<u>But now I do!</u>

First, I have to tell you this: <u>I AM A RUNNER!</u> A sprinter. <u>I run all the time!</u> A sprinter is a person who runs very fast—but only for a short period—like a cheetah, the fastest animal on Earth. I brace my feet against my wooden starting blocks, push off, and keep on exploding—<u>fast!</u>

The All-City Track Meet in 20 more days at George Coleman Poage Park is the *second* thing I have to tell you about. I'm running in four races: the 100 meters, 200 meters, 4 x 100-meter relay, and 4 x 400-meter relay. There are four runners on a relay team. In the 4 x 100, each of us will have to run 100 meters (exactly 109 yards, 1 foot, 1 inch). In the 4 x 400 relay, we will each run 400 meters (437 yards, 1 foot, 4 inches).

The All-City Track Meet is a big deal. Last year our club—Main Track—scored high, but we didn't get first place. We came in second. This year we mean to win <u>big!</u>

I'm captain of the team, which is a little scary but also fun.

Main Track girls are called Gazelles. I gave Coach Teena the name because Wilma Rudolph was called <u>la gazelle</u>—by the Europeans. Today Marie-José Perec, a French sprinter, born in Guadeloupe, is called <u>la gazelle.</u> In the 1996 Olympics, in Atlanta, Georgia, Marie-José won the 400-meter race in 48.25 seconds, an Olympic record. She won gold in the 200 meters, too. But Valerie Brisco-Hooks was the first athlete to ever win back-to-back gold medals in the 200 meters and the 400 meters. That was in Los Angeles, in 1984. In Atlanta, in 1996, Michael Johnson was the first male athlete to win both those medals in one Olympics. He wore gold shoes!

Main Track boys are called Abebes, after Abebe Bikila. He was an Olympic marathon runner from Ethiopia who ran without shoes, and won his first gold medal, in Rome, in 1960. In 1964 he won another Olympic gold medal—for the marathon, again—in Tokyo. A marathon is 26 miles, 385 yards.

Queenie could win a marathon. She is the *third* and last thing I have to tell you about.

Queenie is the new girl. She's one of Ms. Dotty's foster kids, and all she does is show off and talk about how great her <u>real</u> mother was. Her <u>real</u> mother said Queenie was the most perfect daughter in the whole world. That's what everybody's mother says. So what's the big deal? Queenie runs fast. No kidding. She's a long-distance runner, always at top speed!

Her stride is awkward and she doesn't lean forward. Queenie runs looking up at the sky, holding her shoulders lopsided. Her feet look as if they are going to crash into each other. The first time she saw me running at practice, she turned and ran in the other direction! I asked her why she did it. She said, "You were in my way, that's why, and I run where I <u>want</u> to run!"

No matter how clumsily Queenie runs, she is still as fast as I am! Coach Teena says Queenie runs like a sprinter, doesn't conserve her energy. I think Queenie is a show-off and Coach Teena babies her. Last night at practice, Coach Teena screamed at me, her "principal runner." (She has <u>never ever</u> screamed at me.) I tried not to cry. There was a hard lump in my throat that felt like a chunk of track turf. My face was sweaty and my scalp was itching and tears were trying to run out of my eyes.

I'm not mad at Queenie and I'm not mad at Coach Teena, but why did she have to scream? Queenie dropped the baton, not me! My laps were good, my running time was great, and I took the baton from Bunky the way I was supposed to. OK, I was playing around. I ran backward, fell down, and started laughing at my own self. I didn't know Coach Teena was looking. The next thing I heard, she was screaming at me! I couldn't believe it.

Now you know why I need you. I didn't want to show my tears at practice, but

I can show them to you. I felt a chunky-lunky thing in my throat. It's like I was choking and nobody knew. I think Queenie knew, because she looked at me real strange. She didn't come closer, but she didn't move away and laugh, either. Thank goodness!

Aunt Zenzele's coming to All-City. Aunt Zenzele is my father's sister. She used to be my aunt Joyce until she went to court and changed <u>Joyce</u> to an Ndebele name. The Ndebeles are Zulus who live in Zimbabwe. <u>Zenzele</u> means "Do it yourself."

Me and Aunt Zenzele talk about running all the time. She's the one who told me about Louise Stokes and Tidye Pickett. Louise Stokes was a sprinter like me. Tidye Pickett was a hurdler. The two of them qualified for the 1932 Olympic 400-meter relay team, but the coaches made a decision to pull them off the team. They were replaced by two white runners they had beaten in the trials. I wish they had somehow been able to jump into the races and beat those runners again. People would have cheered and screamed, <u>"LOOK AT THEM! WOW!"</u> At the 1936 Olympics, in Berlin, the same thing happened again to Louise Stokes. She was replaced by a white runner she had beaten in the heats. Tidye Pickett didn't make the 1936 U.S. team because she hit one of the hurdles in the semifinals.

"How's my fast-running Rosie?" Aunt Zenzele asked. She laughs and teases me when she says "Rosie." Not many people call me that. Either they say my whole name, Ebonee Rose, or E. R. Most of the time it's E. R.

Aunt Zenzele likes to check me out, make sure I know something—kind of like a test. This morning she called me up and said, "E. R., who is Loroupe?"

Tegla Loroupe. I knew it right away. "New York Marathon winner—1994 and 1995—from Kenya."

"Go on, Ms. E. R.," she said. "What was her 1995 time?"

"Two hours, 28 minutes, 6 seconds," I said. "Fatuma Roba, of Ethiopia, who won gold for the Olympic marathon in 1996, in Atlanta, had the largest margin of victory ever. The silver winner was two minutes behind her!"

My other favorite marathon winner is Loretta Claiborne. She is a gold and silver Special Olympics medalist, and the 1995 Espy Award recipient for Athlete of the Year. In 1991 Runner's World magazine named her Special Olympics Athlete of the Quarter Century.

She is so cool, even when she's not running. After her Espy speech, when the audience gave her a standing ovation, I stood up in my living room. Momma put her arms around me. I was crying, just like some of the people in the audience. Daddy was quiet.

I don't like "Diary." I'm naming you Dee! Florence Griffith Joyner's nickname is Dee Dee. If I called you that, I'd be a copycat! I'm glad Daddy bought you. You're like a secret sister.

Daddy's an investigative reporter. That means he looks for trouble and wrong things; then he reports them in the newspaper. I call him a spy. Did you know spies have deadlines? Momma is a principal, but I am not in her school. Thank goodness!

Jay-Jay, my favorite quarterback and my favorite Abebe, will be at church this morning. He is SOOOO cute! He won't notice my new dress because it doesn't have

FOOTBALLS on it. Jay-Jay plays basketball, too. Just like Wilma Rudolph. But I can't get the ball in the basket no matter how hard I try!

Bye, Dee. It's time to go to church.

E. R.

4:25 p.m.

Sunday
Beneath my feet
No springy clay
My running self
Is still today

I told you Jay-Jay wouldn't notice, and he didn't. I was sitting in the front pew. My Zambian dress is gold and blue, with big puff sleeves and a peplum at the waist like a tutu on a ballerina's costume. I wore white lace stockings and patent leather ankle-strap shoes. Cowrie shells in my hair! Grandpa called me the cat's meow. That means <u>cool</u>.

Jay-Jay's solo was super. His tenor voice sounds tough and sweet at the same time. Everybody clapped. Me, too. I watched the choirmaster when she lifted both her arms high to lead them. It looked like the referee's signal whenever Jay-Jay throws a touchdown pass. I wondered if Jay-Jay noticed. Probably not. He was too busy singing.

Dee, guess what my mother said? She said, "All I ever hear is Jay-Jay!" She was laughing, though. I reminded her that Alice Coachman, the first African American woman to win a gold medal in the Olympics, said, "I used to slip off and go to the playground and play with the boys." I read it in a magazine. Momma just looked at me.

Boys are nice—especially when I race them and win. Or when I try to make them laugh at church, when the boys' choir is singing. The Abebes in the choir were so serious, Dee! They tried not to look at me, but I made them. Only Johnny grinned at me.

Jay-Jay concentrates hard as he sings, just like when he reaches his arm back to throw a pass. Once I called him Chocolate Dimples. He looked at me real hard and said his face didn't come in no candy wrapper. He got mad! If I had dimples, I'd grin all the time.

Coach Teena was in church, too. She wore a thin green-flowered dress. Coach Teena is short and strong. Her soft, curly hair is cut close to her head, except for her bangs. When she screamed at me the other day, a part of her bangs shook. She touched me on the shoulder when she passed my seat. I only smiled a little.

At the end of church service, Coach Teena went to the altar. I think she was praying about All-City. I got up from my seat and knelt close to her. The Abebes and two more Gazelles joined her. She kept her face close to the altar rail. Actually, she's not much taller than the altar rail! When Coach Teena finally stood up, she hugged us. Hugged me tight. I hugged her back. Real hard.

E. R.

Dear Dee,

Queenie called me twice. This is what happened.

"Queenie, why did you call me a second ago and then bang the phone down?"

"So!"

"So? Why are you acting this way?"

"You didn't talk to me Friday at practice."

"Queenie, I tried to talk, but you kept turning away."

"You said I dropped the baton."

"You <u>did</u> drop it. I was trying to help, show you how to pass—"

"You don't know everything!"

"I've passed it wrong plenty of times. Coach Teena would only fuss—"

"I saw her yelling at you. You were getting ready to cry. Next time she yells at you, I'm telling her where to go—"

"No, Queenie!"

"She better not make you sad again."

"It's all right."

"I don't let nobody mess with my friends."

<u>I didn't know we were friends.</u>

Dee, Coach Teena is OK. She's short like Mae Faggs, the youngest member of the U.S. Olympic track-and-field team in 1948. Her nickname is Little Mae, and she is 5 feet 2 inches. That's little!

Here's a story I read about Little Mae. When she was in elementary school, in New York, a policeman came looking for boys to run in a track meet. Little Mae told him that she could outrun all the boys, and she did. Then she ran with a girls' team for the New York Police Athletic League. In 1947 another policeman started an Amateur Athletic Union team and told Little Mae that she would soon be in the Olympics. He was right. She made the 1948 Olympic team, but she placed third in the trials in London. But four years later, in 1952, Mae Faggs won a gold medal for the 4 x 400 relay, in Helsinki, Finland. In 1956 she won a bronze medal for the 4 x 100 relay.

In 1955, when she graduated from Tennessee State University, in Nashville, she was the main star of the T-I-G-E-R-B-E-L-L-E-S! The Tigerbelles were coached by Ed Temple, and they were some of the most famous female runners in American history. Wilma Rudolph was a Tigerbelle—and Wyomia Tyus, Edith McGuire, and Madeline Manning.

I'm going to be a Tigerbelle one day!

See you later, Dee. Momma's ready to run. So am I.

E. R.

"I'd be coming down the straightaway all by myself."
MAE FAGGS

Tennessee Tigerbelle

Run on
Tennessee Tigerbelle
gold/silver/bronze
eagles soar at your heels!

Run on
be swift
celebrate the runners' tale

Mae Faggs (second from right)

Runnin' with Momma
Jumping jacks
we stretch and bend
press our feet
hard against the patio wall

Because trails were opened for us,
we run,
past the pool
out the yard
to renamed streets:
Evelyn Ashford Thoroughfare
Valerie Brisco-Hooks Overpass
Loretta Claiborne Turnpike
Alice Coachman Boardwalk

Gail Devers Esplanade
Mae Faggs Drive
Florence Griffith Joyner Plaza
Jackie Joyner-Kersee Promenade
Madeline Manning Expressway
Mildred McDaniel Passageway
Edith McGuire Avenue
Audrey Patterson Artery
Wilma Rudolph Boulevard
Gwen Torrence Highway
Wyomia Tyus Speedway

Saluting stars,
we turn back
run slower/cool down

9:30 p.m.

Dee,

Momma and I ran back to the house. Before bed, we put beets, carrots, cabbage, and apples into the juicer. We drank two glasses of water and two glasses of our juice. My stomach poked out. "Momma, " I said, "there's only 19 more days before All-City Track Meet."

"That's better than 18," she answered.

Nothing flips her out! She stays cool.

Daddy came into the kitchen and drank two cups of black coffee. Upset me, upset Momma. He loves nasty old ugly caffeine. "Writer's brew," he said. He laughed and went back to his office. Momma leaned against the counter and watched him. She didn't laugh. I put water in the tub and took my bath.

I got out of the tub, cleaned up my bathroom, put you, Dee, under my pillow, and closed my eyes. The phone rang, and it was Queenie. She said Coach Teena said Queenie would be my pacer. A pacer is a person who can help you run at a certain speed. Sometimes she will run the whole way with you and sometimes she won't. A pacer can be a coach or just somebody as fast as you are. The pacer lets you know how you have to run.

Then Queenie said her mother ran faster than anybody.

I told her OK.

"You and your mother ran past here. I saw you. Where did you two get those country-yellow sneakers? They look so dumb!"

"We bought them at a discount store." I was so mad, I had to think for a moment. Then I said, "We like our shoes—sorry you don't."

I hung up the phone and went to sleep.

E. R.

Dream

Last night at sleep's place
a dream knocked on my door
sang bright orange songs
splashed purple on the floor
blue laughed, tickling me
till hurdy-gurdy green
spun an emerald tent
sparkling bright and new.
Oh! I spread my fuchsia wings
and into it—I flew

Chartreuse/scarlet played there
all red and green and yellowy.
I closed my wings
pumped up my feet
and raced them
speedily.

Dee,

This is what happened at practice today. Coach Teena said to me, "If you thought I was screaming at you on Friday because I was angry, I'm sorry. I want you to qualify in your trial heats and then go on and win your races. Your laps looked awfully ragged. Then Queenie dropped the baton and both of you were laughing!" She pointed. "Look in the stands! See those people with video cameras?"

"Yes."

"They're coaches from other teams, seated with their best runners. They're all watching you, Ebonee Rose! You're the one those girls have to beat. Show them what a winner looks like!"

I stood there looking at the crowd. Had they laughed at me the other day? Were they happy to see me making mistakes? Was it difficult to be a coach if you couldn't depend on your principal runner to run a simple lap and do it right? Was it hard to see your star runner playing when she should be concentrating? See her fall backward, lie down on the clay, kick her heels up, and act silly? I felt sad inside, like the petals of pretty flowers were withering inside me. I had let Coach Teena down.

Coach Teena put her arm around me and drew me close. "I'm sorry for screaming," she said. "I have to remember you're not a grown-up, you're a young runner. You're not going to be focused all the time."

"Want to watch me out of the blocks again?" I asked her.

Gwen Torrence

"Yes," Coach Teena said. "And keep the angle of your body low. I want a 90-degree angle on that forward knee. Remember: Project your forward leg off the block for a full extension, E. R. I want to see your long legs stretched all the way out."

I went to my starting blocks. I put a serious look on my face and stirred up the fallen petals inside myself. The petals swirled with energy!

Coach Teena leaned down near my blocks. "This is not only your biggest meet, it's mine, too. And we're <u>not</u> ending up in second place twice in a row!"

"Don't worry, Coach," I said. "You got me."

E. R.

**"I like to see
how fast I can run.
It's fun."**

ROBIN CAMPBELL

Laps

*Grass flattens
beneath my feet—
there is a wind
behind me
pushing
laughing*

*I laugh, too
run faster*

*Wind in front
shoves me back
I lean forward
press harder*

*Wind and I
become friends
run together*

Friday, June 6

Dee,

15 more days before All-City.

Aunt Zenzele spent the night. She said she thought it was Wilma Rudolph who had trouble walking and not Gail Devers. I told her Gail Devers had a sudden case of Graves' disease, which caused her feet to bleed so much she couldn't walk. She had to be carried everywhere, even to the bathroom. Doctors wanted to amputate her feet. That was in 1991. A year later, in 1992, she won a gold medal for the 100 meters at the Olympics in Barcelona, Spain. In the 1996 Olympics, in Atlanta, she won a gold medal for the 100 meters—and another gold medal for the 4 x 100-meter relay. She still has Graves' disease.

Wilma Rudolph had polio, I told Aunt Zenzele. Her left leg was partially paralyzed. She and her mother traveled 200 miles a week on a Greyhound bus to Meharry Medical College, in Nashville, Tennessee, for treatment. Her braces were gone by the time she was 10 years old. Aunt Zenzele said, "Ebonee Rose, I believe you know everything!"

E. R.

Gail Devers

Alice Coachman

Saturday, June 7

Dee,

Did you know Alice Coachman was the first African American woman to win a gold medal in the Olympics and the only American woman to win a gold medal in the 1948 games, in London, England? She won her gold medal for the high jump. She jumped 5 feet 6-1/4 inches. The king of England awarded her medal. In Albany, Georgia, a school is named after her and a street, too!

Audrey Patterson was the first African American woman to ever win a medal in the history of the Olympic Games. She won a bronze medal for the 200-meter race. That was in London, in 1948.

In 1948 my grandmother was 11 years old—just like me!

E. R.

Dee,

Guess what? You won't believe this! I found out that Florence Griffith Joyner <u>writes poetry and keeps a diary!</u>

E. R.

Monday, June 9

Dee,

Can't run with Momma today. This poem will tell you why.

Ankle
Racing
against
my own team

I sprint
to the right—<u>wrong</u>

My ankle
dons
a red dress
takes center stage

Dee,

I was hysterical when my ankle twisted. At first I fell down, and then I jumped up, and then I just sat down and held my whole leg. Coach Teena was trying to get me to at least stop moving, but I couldn't. It hurt too much. How could I <u>hurt</u> myself when All-City is only 11 days away? The buzzing around in my head was—I'm sorry, Coach Teena, I'm sorry, I'm sorry.

Coach Teena wrapped a blue ice pack around my ankle and took me to the hospital. My mother left school and met us in the emergency room.

My ankle was not broken. I had a slight sprain. I worried about All-City. Coach Teena worried about me. Momma said, "What is more important—a track meet or <u>you</u>, Ebonee Rose?"

I wanted to say All-City, but I didn't.

Later Momma said, "We've got a pool at home. It knows what to do with a sore ankle."

That night I prayed. "I HAVE TO RUN!" I said to God. "My team needs me. How long will my ankle be swollen?"

God did not answer.

E. R.

> **"When you are trying to go fast, you are fighting against your body instead of letting go."**
>
> FLORENCE GRIFFITH JOYNER

Dee,

My ankle hurt and I couldn't sleep, so I read my new track-and-field library book again. I found out about Mildred McDaniel. She was a basketball player at David Howard Junior High School, in Atlanta, Georgia. One day, at a high school practice, she kept seeing a girl trying to high-jump. The girl couldn't do it. The coach asked Mildred, "Can you jump it?"

"Sure. I can jump it," she said, and did.

She began to participate in track-and-field events, including the relay team. She won a gold medal in the Olympics for the high jump in Melbourne, Australia, in 1956. Her gold medal was the only one that an American woman won that year. And guess what, Dee? When Mildred McDaniel competed at the 1955 Pan-American Games, she had a sore heel. She won the high-jump title anyway.

So—my dumb ankle's no big deal!

E. R.

Wednesday, June 11

Dee,

My ankle is doing OK. Daddy heated the pool to what Momma called the boiling point. All I know is that the warm water felt good against my ankle. Sometimes I sat on the edge of the pool—my foot in the water—and read my track books.

At practice Coach Teena said, "Great!" But she wouldn't let me run my laps (especially with Queenie pacing me). Queenie's the best pacer I've ever had at Main Track. Too bad she's so mean! She had no business making fun of me and Momma's yellow shoes.

Momma said, "Her mother's dead, E. R., and she doesn't have a family. Try and be a friend to Queenie."

I thought about that for a long time.

Coach Teena is trying to help Queenie not to exaggerate her stride, just run naturally, plain—to conserve her energy, not explode at the very beginning of the 400 meters. Queenie uses a long stride and then she does this strange-looking short stride. I'm not sure which one of us will anchor the relays, but at practice Queenie dropped the baton three times.

Ms. Dotty, Queenie's foster mother, has the biggest yard in the whole neighborhood—and the biggest pool, too. But I found out that Queenie can't tread water.

E. R.

Queenie
She runs
like me
fast/faster
<u>*fastest*</u>

We are rabbits
for each other

23 laps/I want
to stop/fall
"Keep going," she says.
"They think we can't."

Lap 31/we run slow
cool down/talk

Queenie,
maybe someday
we will be
friends

Thursday, June 12

Dee,

    All-City Track Meet is 9 days away.

    My ankle is doing great now, but it was still wrapped when I went to school the other day. The kids were saying, "E. R., what's wrong with your foot? You can't race at All-City?" They were scared for me.

    Last night Momma and I ran for an hour. Daddy followed us in the car. When we

Florence Griffith Joyner

came back, I swam in our pool for a while, exercising my ankle. Then I took my bath and went to bed.

But this running girl can't sleep. If only you were real, Dee, and not just my diary.

Oh! Queenie and I are getting closer and closer. I forgave her for making fun of our yellow shoes. Queenie's mother died and left her, but my mother is alive. If Momma was dead, I'd be so scared.

E. R.

11:30 p.m.

Dee,

Me again. I still can't sleep. Oh, DEE! I forgot to tell you my pictures of Flo Jo came in the mail. Her real name is Florence Delorez Griffith Joyner. The sportswriters call her Flo Jo, and that's what I call her, too.

She's one of the fastest women in the world, and I was so sad when she chose not to compete in the 1996 Olympics, in Atlanta. Momma said, "Be thankful for what she's already given."

In the 1984 Olympics, in Los Angeles, Flo Jo won a silver medal in the 200 meters. In the 1988 Olympics, in Seoul,

Korea, she won a gold medal for the 100 meters, a gold medal for the 200 meters, a gold medal for the 4 x 100-meter relay, and a silver medal for the 4 x 400-meter relay. She ran anchor for the 4 x 400-meter relay.

Can you believe it! Can you <u>believe</u> it!

Dee, her fingernails are long and pretty and all different colors. She cuts off one of the legs from her tights and runs barelegged. Or she'll wear white lace tights. All kinds of tights mixed together. Sharp! Sharp! (Oh, Gail Devers painted her long fingernails <u>gold</u> for the 1996 Games.)

When Flo Jo was a little girl, she used to race jackrabbits in the Mohave Desert. That's why when Queenie paces me, I call her a rabbit. Flo Jo started running when she was 7 years old, 4 years younger than I am now. When she was 14, she won the annual Jesse Owens Youth Games in Los Angeles. She won again at 15. Guess what kind of pet she had when she was in high school? A boa constrictor!

Flo Jo is married to Jackie Joyner-Kersee's brother, Alfrederick (Al) Joyner. He's her coach. He won a gold medal in the 1984 Olympics, in Los Angeles. Isn't that cool? The <u>Jo</u> in Flo Jo means <u>Joyner.</u>

I have to tell you what an anchor is. An anchor is the final

"Passing the baton is one of the most important things to running on a relay team. If a baton is dropped, it is the passer's fault automatically, no matter what happens."
WILMA RUDOLPH
☆ ☆ ☆ ☆ ☆ ☆ ☆

leg of a relay, the fastest runner. The anchor has to overcome any slowness of the other three runners and power on to the end. The lead runner, or lead-off, is the first leg of a relay team. That runner has to be superfast, and confident, too.

The runners in a relay depend on one another to be fast and not make mistakes. Like dropping one of the batons. I'm not mentioning any names, but you know who I mean!

Baton passing is really scary. At the Olympics in Seoul, Korea, in 1988, the women's 4 x 100-meter race had a shaky baton-passing moment— from Flo Jo to Evelyn Ashford! But Evelyn Ashford was the anchor and she overcame it. The team won a gold medal.

E. R.

P.S. I traced my hand on this page. Then I used my markers to make all the fingernails different colors.

Flo Jo and the Jackrabbit

Long-eared
long-legged
hare
run <u>fast</u>

I am
behind you
at your side
in front
now

Good-bye
jackrabbit
hare
good-bye

Florence Griffith Joyner

Saturday, June 14

Dee,

 Momma tells me I have Flo Jo fever. I do have it—but I've got Jackie Joyner-Kersee fever, too. Jacqueline Joyner-Kersee could do everything! Watch this stuff I list: basketball, hurdles, high jump, shot put, the 100 meters, 200 meters, 800 meters,

"I was the underdog, and I was out to win."
VALERIE
BRISCO-HOOKS

long jump, volleyball, triple jump, 1,600-meter relay, and the javelin throw.

Her name is Jacqueline, but it is usually shortened to Jackie. She is a heptathlon champion. A heptathlon is a seven-event track-and-field contest. The seven events are: the 100-meter hurdles, high jump, shot put, the 100 meters, 200 meters, 800 meters, and long jump. In the 1984 Olympics, in Los Angeles, Jackie won a silver medal for the heptathlon. In Seoul, Korea, in 1988, she won gold medals in both the heptathlon and the long jump.

Daddy said she's the greatest female athlete that ever lived, "Except for you, of course, E. R."

At the 1992 Olympics, in Barcelona, Spain, Jackie won a bronze medal for the long jump and another gold medal for the heptathlon. Jackie Joyner-Kersee is the first American woman to win the Olympic long jump and the first athlete in 64 years to win a multievent and an individual event in one Olympics.

The last thing is this: Jackie was second in the heptathlon 100-meter hurdles trial in the 1996 Olympics, in Atlanta—but she ran with an injured right hamstring. (The hamstring is a long muscle at the back of the thigh that helps to flex the knee.) It was raining, and Jackie's face was stretched with pain. I couldn't stand to watch her hurting that much. I hugged Momma hard and kept my face turned away. When Jackie pulled out of the heptathlon competition, she was crying hard. I cried with her. But I was happy she had the courage to withdraw and not compete in pain with an injured body. She was suffering too much. Jackie stayed in the long-jump competition and won a bronze medal for third place. The stadium went nuts clapping for her.

Me, too!

Jackie's 1988 heptathlon score—7,291 points—is still not beaten. In 1992 she scored 7,044 heptathlon points. The 1996 heptathlon gold medalist had a total of 6,780 points.

Got to go now. I have to meet Queenie tomorrow. Ms. Dotty invited me over to

Jackie Joyner-Kersee

celebrate Queenie's "anniversary." She's lived at Ms. Dotty's for a year. We're going swimming in her backyard pool. My ankle doesn't hurt, but maybe it's a little stiff. I'm going to kick and kick and kick in that water!

Coach Teena still hasn't decided who will anchor the team.

E. R.

"The only thing I can say is that I gave 100 percent all the time. . . . I never gave up."

JACKIE JOYNER-KERSEE

☆ ☆ ☆ ☆ ☆ ☆ ☆ ☆ ☆ ☆

Sunday, June 15

Dee,

This is what happened in the water.

"Queenie," I said, "you're not even trying!"

"I am!"

I told her, "Stop holding the ledge—hold me. I won't let you drown."

"I don't want to tread." That's all she kept saying.

"You <u>have</u> to learn," I fussed.

Queenie kept reaching for the ledge, clung to it hard. "I hate deep water."

I stopped treading and went to the edge of the pool. My dark brown shoulder touched her skinny dark brown shoulder. It looked like some of the water on her face was sweat. Queenie was really scared.

Ms. Dotty was sitting on the pool deck, watching all of us. She's helped to train me so I can be a junior lifeguard in a few summers. Queenie wouldn't even let Ms. Dotty teach her to tread water. She kept saying, "I don't want to drown!"

"Ms. Dotty is a lifeguard," I told her.

"I know!" Queenie said. Then all of a sudden she said, "Let's water-race. A fake practice."

We looked at each other and just laughed and laughed. We ran and ran in the water. The water tried to hold us back, but we kept pushing through its force. My ankle was pumped! Not stiff. It felt tough.

"Sorry I made fun of you and your momma's sneakers," Queenie said, but she sounded as mean as ever. We were huffing and puffing. The water had finally beaten us.

I had already forgiven her. "We like yellow," I said. "It looks pretty on us."

"Betcha I drop the baton again," Queenie said, suddenly sad.

"No, you won't," I told her.

"How do you know, Rosie?"

"I just do," I said.

E. R.

Dee,

At the end of practice, Coach Teena came over to me. This is what she said: "Queenie's going to be lead runner in the 4 x 100 meters. You'll anchor, E. R."

<u>I'm glad Queenie didn't drop the baton today,</u> I thought. So, now I know—it's me. The anchor. I have to supply the final power. I will have to overcome the other runners' mistakes, if they make any. I am the last one—and the main one—responsible for winning.

The flower petals in my stomach have begun to flutter, Dee. To shift and drift. I've tried to make them fall back down, to lie flat, but the petals are swirling faster and faster. Can I do it? Can I win? Can I bring the team the victory we want so badly?

"How's that ankle, still OK? Be honest, E. R."

"No problem, Coach Teena," I said truthfully.

"OK, I got you in the 100 meters, 200 meters, 4 x 100-meter relay, and long jump."

LONG JUMP? <u>NO!</u>

"Do I <u>have</u> to long-jump?" I asked her.

"You have to have a field event," she said.

"Yuck! I only want to sprint." The long jump means flying!

"E. R., you have to do a field event, that's the rule," Coach Teena said. "This is a track-and-<u>field</u> meet, remember? Your long jump is pretty good, but we need to work on your takeoff. Also, your heels. Keep your legs together when you land."

Long Jump
I run/lift
my stone body
up/over

Oar-arms
push back
air

I am sailing
out/up/high
flying

Wing-arms
Stretch out/now
for landing

Feet dig in/clutch
the ground/my
weighty flight
stops

Jackie Joyner-Kersee

Dee,

I found out that Jackie Joyner-Kersee set a long-jump record of 20 feet 7-1/2 inches while she was at Lincoln High School in East St. Louis, Illinois, and was state champion. Then she set a record in the 1988 Olympics, in Seoul, Korea. She jumped 24 feet 3-1/2 inches and beat her old 1984 Olympic record of 23 feet 3/4 inch! In the 1996 Olympics, in Atlanta, she won bronze for a jump of 22 feet 11-3/4 inches. I screamed as loud as the people in the stadium!

I wish she was jumping for me in All-City.

E. R.

P.S. At the library after school, my favorite librarian, Ms. Josephine Hobbs-Ford, helped me with my homework. She was Detroit's three-time state champion in track while she was at Detroit's Central High School. She started running when she was 10.

We talked about running, and she told me about her last track meet at Central. The race was 200 meters. There was a girl who usually beat her. Ms. Hobbs-Ford said, "Both of us ran the 200 meters, and she always passed me at a certain time. But this time she didn't pass me. I said to myself, <u>Where is she? Where is she?</u> Then suddenly I knew she wasn't coming, she was far behind, and I told myself, <u>I'm going for it.</u> I won—and my coaches were jumping around so happy. But I was the happiest of all!"

(I wonder if anybody ever made <u>her</u> do the long jump!)

E. R.

Deeeeeeee,

It's Wednesday and I thought my ankle hurt again, no kidding. Momma examined it, Daddy examined it, Coach Teena examined it. But my ankle was not swollen.

"No practice," said Coach Teena.

"No nothing," Daddy said.

"No wanna-be doctors," Momma said. "Let's go."

At the hospital my ankle didn't hurt anymore. The X rays showed nothing. The doctor said he couldn't find any tenderness. "What's up?" he asked me.

"I don't want to do the long jump," I said kind of quietly. I didn't want to fly—I wanted to run.

Momma looked at a blank wall, not at me.

"What <u>do</u> you want?" the doctor asked.

"100 meters, 200 meters, 4 x 100 relay, and 4 x 400 relay. My ankle will hurt if I do the long jump!" I said.

"Uh-huh. What do you think, mother?" the doctor asked Momma.

"Doctor," Momma said, "please don't ask me right this moment. OK?"

The doctor laughed. I liked him. He looked like the pianist Awadagin Pratt.

Momma and the doctor were talking about me, but I was not listening. I do not want to long-jump! Coach Teena thinks I can do everything.

"I can't do the long jump," I said again to Momma and the doctor. "You don't know how hard it is, Momma. You have to fly, and I can't fly a long way yet!"

Momma said, "Try. Do your best." She didn't understand. Maybe she never tried to long-jump. Then I thought, <u>Why not teach Momma how to long-jump?</u>

Right away, Momma liked the idea.

Maybe if I helped her, I could help myself get better. Doing the long jump with Momma would make it kind of cool.

The doctor smiled. He said, "Have you ever heard of Jackie Joyner-Kersee?"

"I love her," I said.

The doctor turned to speak to another doctor in the emergency room.

When he looked back at me, I said, "Her American record for the long jump was 24 feet 5-1/2 inches. Indianapolis, Indiana—1987."

I also told him about Willye White's silver medal, in the 1956 Olympics. She jumped 19 feet 11-3/4 inches.

Then the doctor patted my ankle. "It's fine," he said. "You're going to have a great long jump. When—soon?"

"Saturday," I told him.

"Good luck," he said.

Dee, guess what the doctor called me? <u>Little Encyclopedia.</u>

E. R.

P.S. We run our <u>heats</u> tomorrow. Heats are trials. If I don't place, I don't qualify. If I don't qualify, I can't run.

Only 3 more days before All-City Meet!

Dee,

The crowd at George Coleman Poage Park was huge, and this was just for the heats! (Oh, Dee, I forgot to tell you that George Coleman Poage was the first African American athlete to compete in the Olympics. He won a bronze medal in the 400-meter hurdles. That was in St. Louis in 1904.)

The people in Poage Park were spread out like the tentacles of a giant octopus. Each section was a tentacle of team colors, flashing brightly. Balloons, coaches, parents, cars, and water jugs. Rainbow tentacles shifted and drifted with cries and shouts.

I didn't make any noise. I just sat quiet. All the runners ran laps. We watched each other sneakily, like spies.

Daddy said, "You're really into that spy thing, aren't you?"

We <u>had</u> to be spies. <u>Who will win today? Who will lose in the heats? Will I run badly and not qualify for the team? Does anybody else have a bad ankle? Are any of the principal runners in trouble? Sick?</u>

The day was hot and prickly. The noise and the runners flitting about made me kind of jumpy. I wanted to hurry up and get my heats over with.

I tried to relax, but Queenie pranced around saying she knew <u>nobody</u> in the whole park could beat her! She was bragging and bragging. I'd never ever seen her do that. "I am not wor-RIED," she kept saying over and over. I wondered if that was true.

I could see that Queenie annoyed a few of the other coaches because she kept moving close to their runners, making remarks. "I <u>know</u> you don't think you can outrun me!" she said to a group of little kids who were much younger than she is. Queenie really scared them. I decided she was scared. "Let's you and me walk around and talk," I said.

"Leave me alone, Rosie," Queenie said. "I'm telling you!" But she followed and stayed beside me. We walked all around, never running, just walking and walking. After a while neither of us spoke. It was quiet and nice—just the two of us. She put her arm around me. I put my arm around her. We kept walking.

"I'm scared a little," I finally said.

"Me, too," Queenie said, her skinny arm light against my neck. She looked around Poage Park. "Runners everywhere," she said.

"And we're <u>all</u> fast," I told her.

"Right," Queenie said softly.

Then it was time for me to run my heats. I felt calm. I love to run on a great track. At Poage Park the track is blue, a little darker than the sky on a pretty day. The track felt super under my feet. The only sound I heard was my cleats pounding the spongy turf. I ran faster and faster. The petals inside of me flew straight ahead.

I passed all my heats, <u>even the long jump.</u> Practicing with Momma helped a lot. I've learned how to beat the air back and sail forward. (I still don't really <u>like</u> it, though.)

We Main Track runners passed all our heats. We were yelling and sweating and hugging one another. Momma hugged me the most when I qualified for the long jump. Daddy hugged me, hugged Queenie, hugged Jay-Jay. Coach Teena was happy, too. There were no injuries, she said.

In my room I got down on my knees and prayed like Valerie Brisco-Hooks when she won three gold medals in the 1984 Olympics, in Los Angeles. I prayed for my whole team, and thanked God for Queenie.

She did not drop the baton today.

E. R.

P.S. Guess who I loved in the 1996 Olympics, in Atlanta? Rachida Mahamane from Niger, Africa. She was 14 and competed in the semifinal heat for the women's 5,000 meters. Rachida finished last—more than two laps behind an athlete from Ireland—but she's still a champion to me. She kept going, kept running to the end. I wish I could have run beside her!

"Believe you can . . . and have fun. Just get out there and do it!"
ALICE COACHMAN

7:36 p.m.

Dee,

Jay-Jay called me. He said, "I saw you in church last week watching me sing."

I said, "I was looking at the whole choir."

He said, "I saw you staring!"

"When the girls' choir sings, you look at me, too."

"Use me as an example. When the walls are closing in, when someone doesn't know where to turn, tell people I was there, I kept going."

GAIL DEVERS

He said, "Naw." Then he said, "You did look pretty, Rosie-Posie Main Track Star."

"Thank you." Then I said, "You got the best voice in the boys' choir."

"I know it, I know it, I know it!"

"Puh-leeze," I said. "All you k-n-o-w is football, football, football. You're an Abebe on the track team, but you never talk about track!"

"I don't want a <u>lady</u> coach!"

"You can't run fast, that's why."

"I got a fast arm!"

"Make your legs fast, too," I said.

"<u>Your</u> legs are fast," he told me. "Make sure you win, Rosie-Posie."

"I hope I do."

"You gonna win! Run in that African dress—pretty. Big sleeves, your skinny arms! Cowrie shells all shiny in your hair."

"I'll run in my dress when you play football in your choir robe!"

Boys don't make sense. First they say something nice. Then they say something stupid.

E. R.

DEEEEEEE,

It's 1 day before All-City. I am trying to calm down. I have to write my final language arts essay.

My essay is about families. Wilma Rudolph had 21 sisters and brothers. I don't have any—but she was a runner and so am I. She had a large family cheering her on, and helping her run.

I have a large family, too.

Some of my sisters are: Evelyn Ashford, Margaret Bailes, Kim Batten, Jeanette Bolden, Alice Brown, Earlene Brown, Tonja Buford-Bailey, Chandra Cheeseborough, Alice Coachman, Isabelle Daniels, Gail Devers, Sheila Echols, Mae Faggs, Barbara Ferrell, Michelle Finn, Benita Fitzgerald-Brown, Chryste Gaines, Kim Gallagher, Kim Graham, Carlette Guidry, Catherine Hardy, Sherrie Howard, Martha Hudson, Barbara Pearl Jones, Esther Jones, Jackie Joyner-Kersee, Lillie Leatherwood, Maicel Malone, Madeline Manning, Margaret Matthews, Edith McGuire, Jearl Miles, Inger Miller, Mildrette Netter, Audrey Patterson, Rochelle Stevens, Gwen Torrence, Marilyn White, Willye White, and Lucinda Williams. I will add new names forever.

Robin Campbell

Merlene Ottey, Deon Hemmings, Grace Jackson (Jamaica); Marie-José Perec, Patricia Girard-Leno (France); Denise Lewis (Great Britain); Ana Fidelia Quirot (Cuba); Pauline Konga, Tegla Loroupe (Kenya); Fatuma Roba, Derartu Tulu, Gete Wami (Ethiopia); Chioma Ajunwa, Falilat Ogunkoya, Mary Onyali (Nigeria); Maria Mutola (Mozambique); and Rachida Mahamane (Niger). When I run, they are with me—all my sisters!

My brothers are: Derrick Adkins, Charles Austin, Henry Carr, Joe Deloach, Harrison Dillard, Jon Drummond, Alvin Harrison, Kenny Harrison, Bob Hayes, James Hines, DeHart Hubbard, Allen Johnson, Michael Johnson, Rafer Johnson, Carl Lewis, Mike Marsh, Anthuan Maybank, Derek Mills, Dennis Mitchell, Edwin Moses, Dan O'Brien, Jesse Owens, Butch Reynolds, Calvin Smith, LaMont Smith, Tommie Smith, Andrew Stansfield, John Taylor, Eddie Tolan, and Mal Whitield. They are running at my side—fast, fast.

Also, Donovan Bailey (Canada), Haile Gebrselassie (Ethiopia), Joseph Keter (Kenya), Venuste Niyongabo (Burundi), and Josia Thugwane (South Africa).

We are all runners. We are all connected. We are all family.

E. R.

8:20 p.m.

Dee,

Queenie was sick today at our last practice. She spit up twice. She felt dizzy. She said she didn't want to run tomorrow. The whole team yelled at her. Except me.

I sat down on the bench beside her. Queenie kept holding her stomach and looking at me. "I'm not playing, Rosie. I'm really sick!"

"You might feel better tomorrow," I said.

"I hate tomorrow," she said. "Everybody thinks I'm going to drop the baton. I know that's what they think. You think it, too!"

I didn't answer Queenie; I sat closer and put my arm around her. She said, "Go with me to the rest room again."

I did. Queenie spit up again. She was leaning against the wall. I leaned against the wall, too. "Talk to me, Rosie," she said.

"It's OK to be nervous," I said.

"I'm tense, not <u>nervous."</u>

I told her, "Willye White said if there were no butterflies in her stomach, she didn't feel right. She ran in five Olympics (1956, 1960, 1964, 1968, and 1972). She was lead runner—just like you."

"I don't want to have to run and win and do all this stuff," Queenie insisted, pulling away from me. "I just want to have fun."

"Like Wyomia Tyus," I told her.

Queenie just sat still.

"All I had to do was perform at my best."

WILLYE WHITE

I moved closer and held Queenie tight. She did not pull away. "Just have fun, Queenie," I whispered. "Maybe we'll win the relay."

"I <u>have</u> to win," she said.

"Well, we'll win then," I answered. "There will be golden apples at the feet of our competition." I told Queenie the story of the ancient Greek myth of Atalanta—the hunter who agreed to marry the man who could beat her running. She was tricked by Hippomenes, who dropped golden apples that she paused to pick up. Hippomenes won the race. "Hippomenes might drop golden apples to stop the other runners tomorrow," I said.

"I hope he brings lots of apples," Queenie said.

E. R.

Saturday, June 21

Dear Dee,

All-City Track Meet at Poage Park is over. This is what happened.

Early this morning I thought of Wyomia Tyus. Twice she won gold medals for the 100 meters at the Olympics, back to back: in 1964, in Tokyo, Japan, and

Wyomia Tyus (far right)

in 1968, in Mexico City, Mexico. She was the first athlete ever to do that!

Also, Wyomia Tyus did something else I had to do today—ran anchor for the 4 x 100 relay. In 1968 she won a gold medal for that, too.

I took my bath before Momma and Daddy got up. I pulled on my burgundy-and-gold team shorts, my tank top, and my burgundy socks with the gold letters: GAZELLES. I slipped my feet into old raggle-taggle sneakers,

"[At the 1964 Olympics] I was just a teenager having fun. . . . And then I won the gold medal!"
WYOMIA TYUS

then used a key to attach steel spikes to my black track shoes. I tied the track shoes together by their burgundy-and-gold laces; I hung them around my neck. I painted each of my fingernails a different color: red, pink, green, yellow, orange, blue, purple, turquoise, gold, and burgundy stripes. I took off my socks and sneakers, and painted my toes to match. But I am not Flo Jo. I am Ebonee Rose, Running Girl. I tied my ponytail with burgundy and gold ribbons.

Today I was the fastest runner in the world. I ran for myself. I ran for the <u>Gazelles.</u>

Before we went to Poage Park, Momma and Daddy sat at the breakfast table. They talked about the morning news, but I knew they were thinking about All-City. I sat there and ate a plate of fruit: sliced cantaloupe, honeydew, kiwi, peaches, and whole green grapes. It was 6:30 A.M. I thought about my first race, the 100 meters. I would run it at 10:30 A.M.

Momma and Daddy wore their matching sweatsuits in burgundy and gold. On the back of Daddy's shirt was: EBONEE ROSE'S DADDY. On the back of Momma's shirt was: EBONEE ROSE'S MOMMA. I didn't have my track number then. Coach Teena pinned it on my shirt, front and back, as soon as I got to Poage Park. Coach Teena kissed my cheek when she pinned on my number, 8146. She said, "Run like the cheetah, be graceful as the gazelle" to all the girls on the team, and hugged each of us.

Aunt Zenzele grinned and said, "You go, girl!"

I was ready. The petals within me began to flutter.

E. R.

Momma

Momma sat close to me in the car. She said, "When you were born, your tiny legs were moving so fast—running, I think."

"Suppose we don't win," I said.

"Suppose you don't lose," she said.

"What if I can't run fast enough?" I fussed.

"What if you run too fast?" she fussed back.

I stopped talking, leaned on her.

She stopped talking, leaned on me.

Daddy

Daddy tied the laces of my track shoes too tight, adjusted my number three times. He poured bottled springwater onto his handkerchief and wiped my face. Said, "Don't be nervous, baby." Rubbed the left side of my face twice.

He pulled my socks up straighter, recentered my number, front and back. Retied my shoelaces. He tied the bow on the left bigger than the bow on the right.

Daddy hugged me, patted my back, smiled with a frown on his face. Said this was just another track meet.

Again.

Coach Teena

"This is your race, E. R.!"

"I know."

"How you feel?"

"I like 100 meters."

"Uh-huh."

"I <u>love</u> this dash!"

"That's more like it! You gonna run over the rest of 'em."

"I saw some good—"

"E. R., they're not as fast as you. I told you that before. Showed you on film."

"I know."

"Act like it! Get on your blocks, teach somebody how to run today!"

Starting Blocks

I adjust my wooden blocks. I stretch my legs and look at them, see other legs in my own: Robin Campbell's legs. I remember the words of Robin Campbell's I read in a book: "You've got to believe you're good . . . but other people are good too." (Robin Campbell was in the fourth grade when she joined her school track team. At 14 she beat the Russians in her first international competition, in 1973, in Richmond, Virginia.)

<u>How fast can I run today? I must be both cheetah and gazelle.</u>

My race is about to begin. I straddle my blocks, wait for the command.

"ON YOUR MARK!"

My left leg is in front.

My power leg is in back, ready.

"SET."

I raise my hips, shift my weight over my hands.

"GO!"

100-Meter Dash

I cannot
break free
all the runners
are—_fast_

My skinny
Black legs
get skinnier/longer
stretch/pass/run
to Africa
to Kilimanjaro
to the Pyramids

My
Black spirit legs
run
home

Valerie Brisco-Hooks (foreground)

200 Meters

I look down the track. See Tidye Pickett. See Louise Stokes. Audrey Patterson. Alice Coachman. See Mae Faggs. Mildred McDaniel. Wilma Rudolph. Wyomia Tyus. Willye White. I see Nell Jackson, the first African American head coach of an American Olympic team, in Melbourne, Australia, 1956. I run toward them all.

"Life is competitive, and you must work hard to earn what you win."

LORETTA CLAIBORNE

Relay

Our relay is next. We are holding hands: Queenie, Bunky, Marti, and me. The four of us stand closer, hold tighter. We do not let go. Coach Teena has her arms stretched across our backs.

We start our ritual. First we call out our own names—then say, "Here!" Since this is a relay, we also call out the names of relay gold medalists from the Olympics in Atlanta, in 1996: "Gail Devers!" "Chryste Gaines!" "Kim Graham!" "Carlette Guidry!" "Maicel Malone!" "Jearl Miles!" "Inger Miller!" "Rochelle Stevens!" "Gwen Torrence!" "Linetta Wilson!"

We answer "Here!" for all of them.

Coach Teena called the names of Tidye Pickett and Louise Stokes, the first African American women who took part in the Olympic trials. "Trailblazers!" she said. We answered, "Los Angeles, 1932!" "Berlin, 1936!" Then Coach Teena said, "Nell Jackson!"

Seventeen athletes present. Four could be seen.

This is what happened.

"We are as one."

GWEN TORRENCE

★ ★ ★ ★ ★ ★ ★ ★

Queenie

Queenie is out there—leading. Our crowd is pumped up, screaming. Queenie runs faster than ever, to the passing zone.

She does not drop the baton. She passes it perfectly! Our fans in the bleachers are going crazy. I hear them while I wait in my zone.

Bunky passes the baton to Marti, whose bowlegs are not as long as mine. She runs with power toward me—her bowlegs are like piston rods. Marti hands the heavy wooden tube to me. Anchor. I've got to secure this race, dig in, keep it steady, grip the prize, not let it get away. <u>Anchor.</u>

I take off! This race is mine. Blue track beneath my winged feet. I run through heaven and outrace angels. Wings clap for me. I lean forward, break the tape.

<u>We win.</u>

Queenie and the others ran to meet me. We kept on running around the track.

Audrey Patterson

The officials let us. Our spikes danced on sky blue turf.

THE PRIZE WAS OURS!

We won <u>first place</u> at All-City. My long jump didn't help much. I wanted to be an eagle but couldn't soar high enough. Still, I got a third-place ribbon. I thought I would finish in seventh place.

On the Main Track team bus, we made up all kinds of songs about winning. We got noisier and noisier. None of the grown-ups stopped us—they were singing, too. The loudest song of all, on the bus, was "Happy Birthday," to Jay-Jay. I sang it solo in a silly-willy-nilly way. Definitely off-key. It was fun, fun, fun.

Coach Teena was presented with the huge city trophy. The name MAIN TRACK CLUB will be inscribed on the brass plate beneath the golden track shoe. We get to keep the trophy for one year.

"At last, at last," Coach Teena said. She held the trophy high and reminded us that Audrey Patterson, a great sprinter and coach, believed that being a good athlete isn't only about winning—it means being prepared "physically, mentally and spiritually."

When we arrived back home, Momma and Daddy told me to bathe quickly and put on my new dress from Grandma and Grandpa. We were all going out for a celebration dinner. Aunt Zenzele refused. She said she'd had too many hot dogs with sauerkraut at All-City.

Momma and I bathed and dressed and waited for Daddy. He is a slowpoke. Then he drove around town and couldn't find the new Galaxy Jemison Restaurant, named after the astronaut Mae Jemison. He said, "We're going back home. I'll cook dinner."

"Good," I said. "I want to call Queenie and everybody, and Jay-Jay. So we can talk about All-City! I love my trophies!"

"Oh, we'll definitely call Jay-Jay," Daddy said, teasing me.

Daddy stopped, used the car phone to call Grandma. She sang a sweet little song about running. Grandma was making it up right then and there. She always does that! Grandpa was singing, too.

Daddy pulled into our garage. Momma said, "Ebonee Rose, run ahead and open the door. I've got to put something in the trunk."

"You're just beginning. Young as you are, you can be in two or three Olympic Games."

ALICE COACHMAN,
TO MAE FAGGS, 1948

I opened the door.

"FIRST PLACE, E. R.!" "ROSIE!" "EBONEE ROSE! WE MADE IT THIS TIME!"

My house was filled with Gazelles and Abebes shouting, "We got first place, yay, yay, yay, yay, yay!" Grandma and Grandpa were there, Coach Teena, the whole track team, and the assistant coaches. Burgundy-and-gold banners. Balloons bobbing. A wide sheet cake with a bunch of miniature track shoes! A pair for each of the kids on the team!

"I grew up believing that you always have to put your best foot forward, and that if you fail, you have to try again."

WYOMIA TYUS

☆ ☆ ☆ ☆ ☆

"Grandma!" I said. "In the car, I thought I was talking to you over your house!"

"I know you did, honey," Grandma said.

Grandma's best friend, Ms. Annie Drew, was there in her wheelchair. Her white hair is always a little blue. "Watched you flying today," she said. "Used to do it myself! Had me some good runnin' legs." I like her a lot.

E. R.

Ms. Annie Drew

Once
she jumped broad
jumped long

Fast as a honeybee
she flew

Now
she watches me race
in her swift old chair—

Annie Drew
honeybee
I fly for me
I fly for you

Sunday, June 22

My pal Dee,

　　It was a great party!

　　The whole team slept at my house. Daddy stayed in the family room with the boys and two of the fathers. The girls had the whole upstairs. I wore my old ballerina nightgown. Next morning Daddy made French toast, eggs, and sausages. Jay-Jay ate six slices of toast and five sausages!

Now all my friends have left. I miss them.

Daddy's staring at his computer. He has another deadline. Momma is writing teacher evaluations from her classroom notes.

I put my bathing suit and a towel in my knapsack. I'm going to Queenie's and swim. (That means staying in the shallow end!)

E. R.

3:17 p.m.

Queenie was wearing a kente-design bathing suit. I said, "You're just like Dee."

"Who's Dee?"

"My play sister," I told her.

"Does she run?"

"No."

"Can she tread water?"

"No."

We jumped in at the shallow end of Ms. Dotty's pool. Then Queenie grabbed hold of the pool ledge. "Let's go down to the other end and swim," she said. I followed her.

Ms. Dotty, sitting on the pool deck, watched us. At the deep end Queenie clung to the ledge. She reached for my bony shoulders and dug her fingers into my skin. I didn't care.

"Pedal like you're riding a bike," I said.

She pedaled too fast, staring down at the dark turquoise water. Then she slowed down, let go, and panicked. I grabbed her. Her eyes got big, big.

Then, Queenie held my shoulder with one hand. We kept riding our invisible bikes. She let go, rode a teeny-weeny time alone, grabbed my shoulder again.

"You did it, Queenie!" I cried.

Queenie pedaled easily, held me with one hand. "Everybody thought I'd drop that baton yesterday."

"Not everybody. Not you and me," I said.

We kept riding water. Queenie let go twice, didn't panic. Her kente swimsuit was pretty. Her shoulders bobbed gently in the deep water. Her legs slowed down and found a rhythm I could have clocked if I had wanted to do it. I smiled. I felt glad, tried to look plain, but happiness kept popping out all over my face.

Queenie pushed the water down with her hands, easily. Then she slapped the water and made it spray on my face. I did the same thing back to her.

"Race you to the other end," I said.

We went down to the shallow end and swam.

"I knew I could do whatever it took."
KIM GALLAGHER

"Treading's easy, Rosie!"

"Dee is a fake sister," I told her. "She's really my diary."

"I have my mother's diary, but no pages are left to write on," Queenie said. She leaned against the pool ledge and did not look at me. Her voice was quiet. "I'm not mean, Rosie. I laugh at kids and poke fun—before they do it to me. They always tease me. I hate it!"

"People did that to Flo Jo," I said.

"That's a lie!"

"It is not," I told her. "Flo Jo said, 'Even when I was a little girl, people used to laugh and criticize me.' Those are her exact words!"

"Wish I could tell my mother I didn't drop the baton yesterday."

"She knows," I said.

E. R.

☆ ☆ ☆ ☆ ☆ ☆ ☆ ☆ ☆ ☆ ☆ ☆ ☆ ☆

Dearest Dee,

Queenie is my very sweetest good-pal friend—just like you, Dee. I wish you could walk and talk and run with us. I wish you were real.

Love,
E. R., Running Girl

"Everyone has
different skills,
interests, bodies,
and strengths,
but there are
plenty of sports
to choose from.
Experiment . . .
be patient and
expect a few
false starts."

GAIL DEVERS

☆ ☆ ☆ ☆ ☆

Author's Note

Do you enjoy running? Would you like to participate in competitive races? If so, join a track club at your school or in your community. Contact organizations such as the Junior Amateur Athletic Union, B'nai B'rith (International Office: Washington, D.C.), the Boys and Girls Clubs of America, the Catholic Youth Organization, the International Kids Fitness Association (Richmond, Virginia), the National Alliance for Youth Sports (West Palm Beach, Florida), the National Association for Sports and Physical Education (Reston, Virginia), the Police Athletic League, Special Olympics International (Washington, D.C.), and the Youth Fitness Coalition (Jersey City, New Jersey).

If there is no group to promote young track-and-field athletes near you, lobby adults in your community to start one.

Racing is exciting! *How fast can I go? How far?*

The joy of running is universal.

Have fun!

Acknowledgments

The author wishes to thank the following individuals for research assistance: Thomas Kevin Allen, Sue Baldus, Dan Batts, Joan Carroll, Pete Cava, Benjamin Davis, Dorothy J. Davis, Michael Dickson, Jamila Joy Garrett, Shirley Edwards Gross, Ruth C. Hayes, Jacqueline Hobbs-Ford, Betsy Hundert, Marylouise J. Isbell, Ernest B. James, Lillie B. James, Brenda Johnson, Betty Gladden Jones, Patricia A. Keith, Kenneth Lewis, Paula Moroz, William P. Moultrie, Carol Nick, Barbara Norfleet-Snell, Elaine Pickeral, Faye Powell, Terracita Powell, Tom Repenning, Jill Schoeniger, Janet Sims-Wood, Loretta Singleton, Eva Slezak, Teresa Stakem, Olivia Swinton, Evelyn Tchiyuka, Myrtle W. Williams, and Judy Zvonkin.